A CROW'S JOURNEY

David Cunningham

Albert Whitman & Company • Morton Grove, Illinois

Dedicated to all children
who have wished for wings
to explore beyond their reach.

Library of Congress Cataloging-in-Publication Data

Cunningham, David, 1938-
A crow's journey/David Cunningham, [author & illustrator].
p.   cm.
Summary: A crow makes a journey to find out what happens to the winter snow.
ISBN 0-8075-1356-3
[1. Crows — Fiction. 2. Water — Fiction. 3. Stories in rhyme.] I. Title.

PZ8.3.C9165Cr   1996   95-35811
[Fic]—dc20   CIP
                                                      AC

The text typeface is Lilith.
The illustrations were done in gouache.
Designed by David Cunningham and Lindaanne Donohoe.

A wandering crow
    was curious to know:
Where does it go,
    this mountain snow,
        each spring?

Mountain snow melts.
Everything is still...

until the water
trickles downhill.

Beneath the pines
and listening thrush

a shallow brook
begins to rush.

The rapid water
runs strong and clear,

wearing rough stones
smoother each year.

On the current
a leaf is drawn

to the waterfall—
then it's gone!

In a trout pool
beyond the spray

calm water collects,
then ripples away.

The restless stream
leaves forest shadows

for a sunlit path
through open meadows.

Soon the stream
turns river size

and bank to bank,
reflects the skies.

Ahead with ease
the water bends

past a village
where the journey ends.

Here the river
mouth spreads wide

and finally meets the ocean tide.

And now the crow is satisfied.

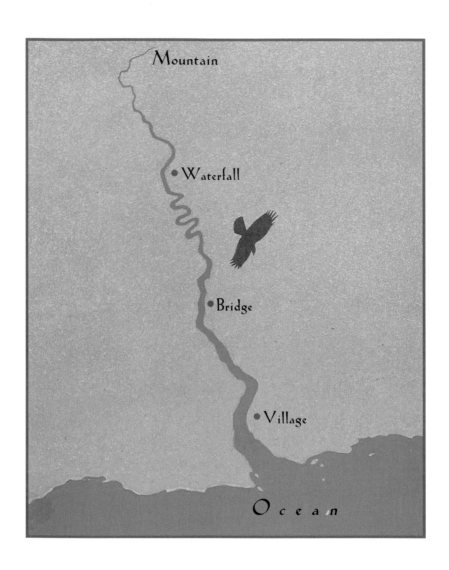

Mountain

• Waterfall

• Bridge

• Village

O c e a n